GROVER SLEEPS OVER

By Elizabeth Winthrop / Illustrated by Maggie Swanson

Featuring JIM HENSON'S SESAME STREET MUPPETS

A SESAME STREET / GOLDEN PRESS BOOK

Published by Western Publishing Company, Inc. in conjunction with Children's Television Workshop.

Grover was packing his overnight bag. The next day
he was going to Betty Lou's house to sleep over. He
had never spent the night away from home before.

Grover packed all the things he wanted to take to
Betty Lou's house: his red fire-truck pajamas; his blue
toothbrush and his striped toothpaste; his furry blue
stuffed monster; his goldfish in a bowl; his begonia in a
flowerpot; his cereal bowl and box of Monsterberry
Crunch; and his night light.

There were too many things to fit into his suitcase.
"Mommy!" Grover called. "I think that I need a bigger suitcase."

"Oh dear, Grover," his mommy said. "You cannot take all of this to Betty Lou's house."

"But Mommy, who will feed my goldfish?" Grover
asked.

"I will," said his mommy.

"Who will water my begonia?" asked Grover.

"I will," said his mommy. "And you won't need your
cereal bowl and Monsterberry Crunch and night light at
Betty Lou's, either."

"But what if Betty Lou doesn't have any Monsterberry Crunch at her house?" asked Grover.

"She will have something else good for breakfast," said his mommy.

"What if Betty Lou doesn't have a night light?" asked Grover.

"I'm sure that Betty Lou has a light in her room that she will leave on for you," Mommy answered.

"Sometimes Ernie tells Bert scary ghost stories at bedtime," said Grover. "Do you think Betty Lou will tell me scary ghost stories?"

"Not if you do not want her to," said Grover's mommy. And she kissed him good night.

The next day Grover's mommy walked with him to Betty Lou's house. When they got there, she kissed him good-by. "I'll see you tomorrow morning when you come home," she said.

"Hi, Grover!" said Betty Lou. "I'm so excited. I've been waiting for you all day. Come in and I'll show you my room."

"Here is your bed," said Betty Lou. "And here are a towel and a washcloth for you."

"Thank you, Betty Lou," said Grover. But he did not put down his suitcase.

"There's something I'd like to ask you, Grover," said Betty Lou. "Is it all right with you if we leave a light on? I like to sleep with a little light on at night."

"Oh, that is just fine with me," said Grover. "I think that I will unpack my suitcase now."

Then Grover put his pajamas under his pillow and his little furry blue monster on top of it.

Betty Lou showed Grover where to put his toothbrush and toothpaste in the bathroom.

After a nice dinner of spaghetti and meatballs and
salad and milk, Betty Lou showed Grover how to feed
her turtle. Then they built a tall tower with blocks.

Betty Lou and Grover played until Betty Lou's mother
said, "Time to get ready for bed."

When Grover and Betty Lou had brushed their teeth and put on their pajamas, Betty Lou's mother tucked Betty Lou in and kissed her good night. She tucked Grover in and kissed him good night, too, just the way his own mommy always did. Then Betty Lou's mother turned on a night light in the corner of the room.

"Grover?" Betty Lou whispered after her mother had left the room. "Are you still awake?"

"Yes," said Grover.

"Ernie tells Bert scary ghost stories before they go to sleep," she said. "Do you know any scary ghost stories?"

"Well, not exactly," said Grover. "Do you know any scary ghost stories?"

"No," said Betty Lou.

"Oh, that is all right. Then we do not have to tell them," said Grover. "Good night, Betty Lou."

"Good night, Grover."

The next morning Grover woke up because he felt something tickling his nose. When he opened his eyes, he didn't know where he was at first. Then he saw what had awakened him. It was Paws, Betty Lou's kitten. Grover looked around the room and remembered that he was at Betty Lou's house.

After Grover and Betty Lou ate breakfast, they played
school. They took turns being the teacher.
Then they painted pictures until it was time for
Grover to pack his suitcase again and go home.

Grover's mommy was waiting for him when he got home. She gave him a big hug and a kiss. "Did you have a good time at Betty Lou's house?" she asked.

"Oh yes, Mommy!" said Grover. "Betty Lou let me feed her turtle, and we built a whole neighborhood with her blocks, and we played school, and guess what!"

"What, Grover?"

"We had Blueberry Chew for breakfast, and I liked it almost as much as Monsterberry Crunch!

"And guess what else!" said Grover. "Betty Lou's mommy invited me to sleep over at their house again very soon—and I cannot wait to go!"